THE
CANDY
MAN

STEVE BRADLEY

A PACEMAKER BESTELLERS™ BOOK

FEARON·PITMAN PUBLISHERS, INC.
Belmont, California

Series Director: Tom Belina
Designer: Richard Kharibian
Cover and illustrations: Warren Lee

ISBN–0–8224–5265–X

Library of Congress Catalog Card Number: 77-78812

Printed in the United States of America.

1. 9 8 7 6 5 4 3 2 1

CONTENTS

CHAPTER **1**

THE BLUE FLIGHT BAG

The bus stopped. The young woman picked up her suitcase. She got off the bus and looked around the Chicago airport. The place was so big!

And there was so much noise.

Jets screamed in the sky above her head.

Soon she would be on one of those jets herself. She couldn't wait! She felt as if she could fly all by herself. She was very happy.

She went inside to the ticket desk.

"My name is Peg Johnson," she told a man behind the desk. "I'd like to pick up my ticket, please."

The man smiled at her. He looked at a list of names on a paper on his desk.

"I have your ticket right here," he said. "A round trip ticket to New York City."

He wrote something on the ticket. Then he gave it to Peg. She paid him for it.

"Your jet leaves in 45 minutes," the man said. "It will be at Gate Ten. You can board in a few minutes. I hope you'll have a nice trip."

"I'm sure I will," Peg said with a smile. She put her ticket in her coat pocket. She walked over to Gate Ten.

Soon, she thought. Soon—in just 45 minutes—I'll be high up in the sky. I'll be on my way to New York City! She looked at the clock on the wall. The clock's hands didn't move fast enough for her.

She heard a telephone ring at the ticket desk.

Another phone rang—this one was in her mind. She remembered her brother Bob's telephone call to her.

"It's your birthday present," he had said to her. "Hope you like it."

"A trip to New York City?"

"On me."

"I don't believe it! Are you sure you want to do this, Bob?"

"Never wanted to do anything more."

"You want to know something? You're the best brother any girl ever had. And I love you."

"Well, you're the best kid sister I could ever hope to have. Even if we did fight like cats and dogs when we were little."

Then they talked about what they would do in New York.

Peg would stay in Bob's apartment. They would go to Radio City Music Hall. They would ride the boat to Staten Island. He would take her out to dinner every night.

And now, Peg thought, here I am. In a few minutes, I'll get on the jet and—

Just then someone bumped into her. She dropped her suitcase.

"I'm so sorry," the man who had bumped into her said. "I wasn't looking where I was going." He looked back across the room. He seemed very nervous. In his hand was a blue flight bag.

"That's OK," Peg said. She was about to pick up her suitcase.

"Let me," the man said. He picked up her suitcase and gave it to her. "I really am very sorry," he said.

"I'm sure you couldn't help it," Peg said.

"Is the New York City jet ready yet?" the man asked.

"Not yet. But it will be soon. Are you going to New York City, too?"

"Yes, I am. On—on business." The man looked around. "Dear me," he said, "I do wish that jet would come."

Peg smiled. Now she knew who the man looked like. He had red cheeks. His hair was white but there wasn't much of it. His eyes were as blue as the sky. He made Peg think of Santa Claus.

"Dear me," the man said again. "I wonder what I did with it?" He put his hand in one of his pockets. Then in another one.

"Is something wrong?" Peg asked him. She smiled again because she had almost called him Santa Claus.

"My ticket," the man said. "I do believe I've lost my ticket."

"No, you haven't lost it," Peg said. "It's right there."

"Where?"

Peg reached out. She took the ticket from the man's top coat pocket.

"Why, thank you, my dear!" the man said. "Thank you ever so much. For a minute there, I was sure that I had lost it."

He looked around again, still very nervous. "Is the jet ready yet?"

"Not yet. But it will be soon."

The man took a paper bag out of his pocket. "Would you like a piece of candy?"

Peg took one. So did the man.

Suddenly, a man ran up to them. He grabbed the man's arm and said, "Give me that flight bag! Hand it over!"

"No!" the man said. "It's mine."

"It isn't yours," the second man said. "You switched bags on me. Mine was the same color as yours. I've been looking all over for you. Now give me back my bag."

"Help!" the man with the white hair shouted. "Someone—please help me!"

Peg didn't know what to do. For a second she just stood there. But then she saw a policeman across the room. She ran over to him. She told him what had just happened.

Peg and the policeman ran toward the two men. The man with the white hair held on to the blue flight bag. The other man tried to pull it out of his hands.

But when he saw the policeman, he ran out of the room.

The policeman and Peg reached the man with the white hair.

"Are you OK?" the policeman asked him.

"Yes, I am," the man answered. "I mean I think I am."

"What was the trouble?" the policeman asked.

"Nothing," the man answered. "Nothing at all important. Thank you very much for your help. And thank you too, young woman," he said to Peg.

"I'll go and look for that other man," the policeman said.

"Have a piece of candy before you go," the man with the white hair said. He held out his bag of candy.

"No, thank you," the policeman said. He left.

"Our jet is here now," Peg said to the man.

"I'm so glad!" he said. "Shall we go, my dear?" He held out his arm. Peg took it.

Together they walked to the jet's door.

CHAPTER **2**

WHAT'S GOING ON HERE?

Once inside the jet, Peg and the man took seats side by side.

"My, isn't this nice," said the man. "I'm so glad to be here at last. Now I feel safe."

"That man in the airport," Peg said. "What—?"

"Let's not talk about him. I get nervous when I even *think* about him."

"I understand," Peg said.

The man reached out and touched her hand. "You're really very nice, my dear. By the way, my name is Baxter. Henry Baxter."

"Mine is Peg Johnson. I'm very glad to meet you, Mr. Baxter."

"Why are you going to New York, my dear?"

"I'm going to visit my brother Bob. He lives in an apartment on East End Avenue. 500 East End Avenue. Do you know it?"

"Yes. That's right by the river, isn't it?"

"Yes, it is. It's really very nice there he tells me. I can't wait to get there. To see my brother, I mean. I haven't seen him in a long time."

"A vacation?" asked Mr. Baxter.

"Yes, in a way. Tomorrow is my birthday. This trip is Bob's birthday present to me."

"How nice."

"It is, isn't it? You see, I've never been to New York before. Bob knew I wanted to visit the city. So he called me up and—well, here I am."

"Your brother must be a very nice person," Mr. Baxter said.

"He is," Peg said. She watched Mr. Baxter take the bag of candy from his pocket. He put a piece of candy in his mouth.

Mr. Baxter saw Peg watching him. "I know I should not eat so much candy," he said. "But I just can't seem to help it. I do love it so!"

At that minute, the jet moved out. Minutes later, the engines roared and then it took off.

"Here we go!" Mr. Baxter said. "I can't wait to get to New York."

"Have you been there before?" Peg asked as they flew up into the sky.

"Yes, often. My business takes me there."

"What business are you in, Mr. Baxter?"

"I'm a salesman."

Mr. Baxter's answer didn't tell Peg much. She decided not to ask him any more questions.

Some time later, lunch was brought to them. They ate. Then Peg read a book she had brought with her.

Mr. Baxter went to sleep. In his hands was his blue flight bag.

Peg decided to take it from him. She would hold it for him. Then he could sleep better.

But, as she tried to take the bag from him, Mr. Baxter woke up.

"What are you doing?" he shouted at Peg. "What do you think you're *doing?*"

"I was just going to—"

"Oh. It's only you," Mr. Baxter said. "I thought someone was going to steal my bag."

"I was just going to hold it for you," Peg said.

"Never mind, my dear. I'll hold on to it. It isn't in my way."

Peg went back to her book. Mr. Baxter looked out the window. He kept his hands on his flight bag.

Some time later, the jet landed in New York.

Peg and Mr. Baxter got off the jet. They both went to the building where Peg would find her suitcase. While they waited for it, Mr. Baxter looked all around.

Peg noticed that he seemed nervous again.

Soon she got her suitcase. "I'm going to take a taxi into the city," she said to Mr. Baxter. "Would you like to ride in with me?"

Mr. Baxter didn't seem to hear her question. His eyes had become very wide.

There is something wrong with him, Peg thought.

"Mr. Baxter," she said. "Mr. Baxter. Is there something I can—?"

"Yes," he whispered. "There is something you can do for me. Will you get me a drink of water, please? Give me your coat. I'll hold it for you. Here."

Peg's coat had been over her arm. She gave it to Mr. Baxter. She walked across the room. She took a paper cup from the machine on the wall. She began to fill the cup with water.

When it was full, she went back to Mr. Baxter. He looks bad, she thought. Was he sick? she wondered. She gave him the water. He gave her back her coat.

Mr. Baxter seemed to be looking hard at something. Peg noticed a man across the room. The man seemed to be watching them. She looked back at Mr. Baxter. He was looking at the man. And he was nervous.

"Mr. Baxter," Peg said. "Are you—?"

But he didn't answer her. Instead, he walked away from her.

"Mr. Baxter!" Peg called out to him.

But he didn't speak to her or turn around. He just kept on going. He turned a corner and was gone from sight.

He didn't even drink the water I brought him, Peg thought. That's funny. Because he did ask for it.

She decided she would wait for him. Perhaps he really was sick. When he felt better, he would come back.

She sat down. When she did, she noticed Mr. Baxter's blue flight bag. It sat on the floor at her feet. He forgot it, she thought.

Now that *really* is funny, she thought. Up until now, he wouldn't let it out of his hands for a minute. She picked up the bag. What's going on here?

As she did so, the man Mr. Baxter had been looking at ran up to her. Before she could speak or move, the man grabbed the flight bag. He pulled it out of her hands. Then he ran across the room and out the door.

Peg ran after him. But she couldn't catch him. He got away.

She went back to where she had left her coat and suitcase. She sat down again. What could she tell Mr. Baxter when he came back? What would he say when she told him his flight bag was gone? Would he believe her if she said a man had taken it from her?

She decided she should tell someone about what had happened.

She went over to the ticket office. She told the woman behind the desk about the flight bag and the man who had taken it. The woman said she would report the matter to the airport police. Peg thanked her.

She went back and sat down. She waited for Mr. Baxter to return.

But he never did.

Finally, Peg decided that she would have to leave without him. If she didn't leave, Bob would worry about her. And Mr. Baxter could always find her if he wanted to. He knew her name. She had told him where Bob lived. She had said she was going to Bob's apartment.

She stood up. She picked up her coat and suitcase. Then she went outside the building. She got into a taxi.

The driver asked her where she wanted to go.

"To 500 East End Avenue," she told him.

Just then, Mr. Baxter came out of the building.

Peg didn't see him. She didn't see him watch her taxi drive away.

She didn't see the strange smile on his fat face either.

CHAPTER **3**

500 EAST END AVENUE

As the taxi came close to New York City, Peg looked out through its windows.

Up ahead of her was the city. Its tall buildings were like stone flowers. They seemed to grow toward the sky.

The sun made the windows of the buildings shine. To Peg, the windows looked like empty eyes. They were, she thought, watching her as she came close to them.

The thought made her nervous. Don't be silly, she told herself. Those are just buildings. And windows are only windows. They are not empty eyes. So stop it!

Then the buildings were all gone. The taxi had gone into a tunnel. Above them now, Peg knew, was the Hudson River. The taxi passed a sign on the wall. It said: New York.

I'm *here,* Peg thought.

Soon the taxi came out of the tunnel. It drove through the streets of New York.

There were people all over the place—lots of them. There were shops, hundreds of them. The streets were full of cars.

The taxi stopped. Red light. Then it started again. Green light. Then it stopped again. Red light.

Hurry, Peg said to herself. Please hurry up.

The taxi stopped again. Peg paid the driver. She got out of the taxi and put her suitcase down.

She looked at the building in front of her. The number over the door was 500. But, just to be sure, Peg looked at the street sign. The sign said: East End Avenue.

She went inside the building. She got on an elevator. She pushed the button for Bob's floor. When the elevator stopped, she got out of it. She went down the hall and stopped in front of a door. She rang the bell.

The door opened.

"Bob!" Peg said.

"Hello, there!" Bob said to her with a big smile. "I thought you would never get here. You're late, aren't you?"

He put his arms around Peg.

"I guess I am a little late," she said. "Bob, it's so good to see you!"

"Come on in," he said. "I'll show you the apartment."

Bob was as tall as Peg. They both had the same dark hair. But Bob had dark eyes. Peg's were light.

"Put your suitcase over there," he told her. "This is the living room."

"It's not very big," Peg said, looking around. "It's not like home."

"No, it's small. It's like New York living rooms. Little room for lots of money."

They both laughed.

He showed Peg the one bedroom in his apartment. "You will sleep in here."

"Where will you sleep?"

"In the living room. Now tell me. How was your trip? You know something? You look just great!"

"The trip was fine," Peg said. "But something happened."

"Sit down and tell me about it," Bob said. "I'll make something for us to eat."

"Not for me," Peg said. "I'm not a bit hungry."

"OK. So tell me what happened."

"Well, I met this man," Peg said.

"That's no surprise to me. A beautiful girl like you—"

"Wait, Bob. Let me tell you about him. He was a nice old man. Well, he wasn't *really* old. But sort of old, if you know what I mean."

She went on to tell Bob what had happened at the Chicago airport. She told him about Mr. Baxter's love for candy. Then she told him that Mr. Baxter had just gone away after they got to New York.

"Here today," Bob said, laughing. "And gone tomorrow."

"Now stop that," Peg said to him with a smile. "I wonder if something happened to him. Really."

Then she told Bob about the other man. The one who took Mr. Baxter's flight bag from her.

"You couldn't help that," Bob said. "Don't worry about it."

"But I do worry about it," Peg said. "There must have been something important in that bag. Mr. Baxter wouldn't let go of it for a minute. Not one minute. And I told you that a man in Chicago—"

"I know," Bob cut in. "A man in Chicago tried to steal the bag."

Peg said, "Yes. And *that* man said the bag was *his* bag."

"Well, I still say it's nothing to worry about," Bob said.

"Maybe it isn't," Peg said. "But I'm sorry it happened."

"Listen," Bob said. "If your candy man wants his bag, he can go to the police about it."

"Candy man?"

"Mr. Baxter," Bob said. "You said he always ate candy."

"Mr. Baxter, the candy man," Peg said and laughed. "No wonder he was so fat."

"Forget about him," Bob said. "Think about New York. Think about the good times we are going to have. Get ready to enjoy your birthday present."

"New York City is the best birthday present I ever had," Peg said. "And I thank you for it."

"Why don't you put the things in your suitcase away now? Then you can wash up. After that, I'll take you out to dinner."

"That sounds fine," Peg said. "It won't take me long to get ready."

She left the room with her suitcase in her hand and went into the bedroom.

She took her clothes out of the suitcase. She put them all away. Then she washed up.

When she came back to the living room, Bob said, "Would you like a drink? I have some nice white wine."

"I'd love some."

Bob gave her a small glass of wine. He took one for himself. He lifted his glass. "To you," he said to Peg.

Peg smiled at her brother.

They drank.

Bob turned on the radio. They listened to some soft music.

Peg drank a little bit of her wine. She put her head back on the soft chair in which she sat. She closed her eyes.

"You're not going to sleep, are you?" Bob asked her.

She shook her head. "No, just taking it all in. It's all so nice," she said. "The music. The wine. I just want to enjoy it."

Suddenly, the door bell rang.

"Now who could that be?" Bob said. He put down his glass of wine. He stood up. He went to the door and opened it.

A man stood outside in the hall. He pushed the door wide open. He pushed Bob out of his way and came into the apartment.

"Wait a minute, you!" Bob yelled. "Where do you think you're going?"

The man turned. He hit Bob in the face. Bob fell back against the door.

The man went over to Peg. He grabbed her arm. "Hello there, Peg Johnson," he said to her.

For a minute, Peg couldn't speak. Then she said, "How do you know my name?"

The man didn't answer her question. Instead, he said, "Give me the statue."

"Statue?" Peg said. "What statue?"

Bob tried to jump the man. But the man stepped out of the way and hit Bob on the back of the neck. Bob fell to the floor.

"Give me the statue," the man said to Peg.

"I don't have any statue," she told him. "I don't know what you're talking about. That's the truth."

"If you don't give me the statue," the man said to her, "you will be sorry. Very, very sorry."

CHAPTER **4**

THE STATUE

Peg tried to fight the man. But he was too strong for her. She was about to give up. Then she noticed her wine glass. It was on the table beside her.

She reached out and picked up the glass. She threw the wine in the man's face.

He let out a yell and let go of Peg. He put both of his hands up to his eyes.

Bob saw his chance. He made a grab for the man's legs. He pulled them toward him. The man gave another yell as he fell down. His head hit the floor with a bang.

He didn't move.

"He's out like a light," Bob said to Peg. "Are you OK?"

"My arm hurts," she said. "But other than that—yes, I'm OK. Did he hurt you?"

Bob shook his head. "Who is he?"

"I don't know."

"You don't know? But he knew your name. Peg, are you sure you don't know him?"

"I never saw him before in my life," Peg said. "I don't know how he knew my name. What shall we do now?"

"Call the police," Bob said. He went over to the telephone.

"What if he wakes up before they get here?" Peg said.

Bob stopped. "You're right. We had better tie him up. I don't have any rope. But we can use the wire from that lamp over there."

"I'll get it for you," said Peg. She walked to the lamp. As she went past the man on the floor, his eyes opened.

"Bob!" Peg said. "He is—"

Bob made a move toward the man. But the man was too fast for him. He got to his feet. He made a grab for Bob.

Bob hit the man once, then again.

The man hit him back.

Peg screamed.

She ran out into the hall. She screamed again. She called for help.

Apartment doors opened. People came out into the hall.

Everyone talked at once.

"What's wrong?"

"Who screamed?"

"Help!" Peg shouted. "There is a man in there." She pointed to Bob's apartment. "He is going to kill my brother."

The man in the apartment heard what she said. He saw the people in the hall. All at once, he ran out of the apartment, pushing people out of the way. He ran down the hall. When he came to the steps, he ran down them.

Peg ran back into the apartment. "Bob!"

He held up a hand. He tried to speak. At first, he couldn't. Finally, he could talk.

"I'll be OK in a minute," he said. He sat down on a chair.

Peg went to the door of the apartment. She looked at all the people in the hall. "Thank you," she said to them. But she was mad.

She was mad because not one of the people had tried to help her or Bob. They had just watched.

She shut the door on them.

"Why didn't they help us?" she asked Bob.

"People are like that here," he answered. "They are afraid to help other people in trouble. They are afraid they might get hurt themselves."

"That's not the way it is back home," Peg said, pushing the hair out of her eyes. "Back home people would all try to help you."

"I guess they can't help it if they are afraid," Bob said. "There are a lot of things to be afraid of in a city like this."

"*I* was afraid," Peg said. "Plenty afraid. But I tried to help you."

"And you did a good job of it," Bob said. "That business with the wine—that was smart."

Peg went to the window and looked out. She didn't say anything.

"Peg? What are you doing?"

"Thinking. About what we should do."

"So am I," Bob said.

Peg turned away from the window. "The police," she said. "We should go and tell them what just happened. Because it could happen again."

"OK," Bob said. "Let's go to the police. But what I don't understand is—"

"*Why* it happened, right?"

"Right," Bob said. "I mean you said you never saw that man before."

"No, I didn't," Peg said. "But he knew my name. And he thought I had a statue that he wanted. But I don't have any statue."

"Are you sure you don't?"

"I took all my things out of my suitcase," Peg said. "There wasn't any statue in my suitcase. So where could it have been?"

"If there really *is* a statue, you mean."

Suddenly, Peg ran out of the room. She picked up her coat which was on the bed. She put her hands in her coat pockets.

She found a small statue in one of her coat pockets. She took it into the living room.

"This must be what that man wanted," she said to Bob. She held up the statue so that he could see it. "It was in my coat pocket."

They both looked at the statue. It was about seven inches tall and rather thick. It was a statue of George Washington. It was painted red, white, and blue.

"It isn't very heavy," Peg said. "I guess that's why I didn't know it was in my coat pocket."

"But how did it get into your coat pocket?" Bob asked.

"I haven't any idea," Peg answered.

"Maybe someone put it there."

"But why would someone do that?" Peg asked. "You can buy statues like this in any ten cent store. They sell them all over the country."

"So why did that man want the thing?" Bob asked. He sounded as if he were talking to himself.

"Let's go to the police," Peg said. "Let's give them the statue. Let them worry about it."

"I suppose that's the best thing to do," Bob said. "I'll get my coat."

When Bob was ready, he said, "We can ride the subway to the police station. We can get the subway at the corner."

They went out into the hall. They rode down on the elevator. Once outside, they walked down the street.

They came to the subway and went down the steps. At the bottom of the steps, Bob gave Peg a token. They both put their tokens into the machines. Then they went to the subway platform to wait for a train.

"How far away is the police station?" Peg asked her brother.

"It's not far. We only have to ride for two stops. It will take us only minutes to get there."

"I hope the train comes soon," Peg said. "I won't feel safe until I give this statue to the police."

Just then, a man came down the subway steps. It was the man who had been in Bob's apartment.

Peg and Bob didn't see him. They were looking down the track for the train.

With the man was another man. A fat man. He had a bag of candy in his hand. He ate a piece of candy.

He said to the other man, "I don't care what happens to the girl. Or to her brother. But I want that statue."

"I'll get it for you this time for sure," the man said. "You can count on it."

He began to walk toward Peg and Bob.

CHAPTER **5**

WON'T ANYONE HELP?

The two men put tokens into the machines. They went out on the subway platform. They moved through the crowd of people on the platform.

Peg turned around. At first, she didn't see the two men. But then she did see them. She put her hand on Bob's arm.

"What is it?" he asked her.

"Bob! We have to get out of here," she said in a low voice. "Look!"

Bob looked. He saw the man who had been in his apartment.

"Who is that with him?" he asked Peg.

"That's Mr. Baxter," she said. "He is the man I told you about. The man I met in the Chicago airport. The one who went away and didn't come back. It was his flight bag that was taken from me."

"The candy man?"

"Yes," Peg said.

"We will have to make a run for it," Bob said. "Are you ready?"

"No," Peg said. "I'm not really ready. But I guess I had better get ready, right?"

"You run that way," Bob told her. "I'll go around them on the other side. One of us will get past them. The one who does can find a policeman and bring him back here."

"Won't any of these people help us?" Peg asked. She looked at the people on the platform. "Won't anyone help?"

"Don't count on it," Bob said. "Let's *move!*"

They both ran toward the two men. Peg ran to the right, Bob to the left.

The man with Mr. Baxter made a grab for Peg. But she got past him.

He ran after her. He cut her off. He forced her to run back the way she had come.

Bob saw what the man had done. He ran back to help Peg.

Mr. Baxter watched. So did all the people on the platform.

Bob pushed people out of his way. One of the people he pushed bumped into the man who was after Peg. That slowed the man down.

Bob caught up with Peg.

They were at the far end of the platform. Bob looked around. So did Peg.

"Where can we go from here?" she asked. "We can't go back the way we came. They will catch us if we do."

Bob looked down at the train tracks. Then he said, "There is only one thing to do—one place to go. It's the best we can do if we want to get away. We have to go down there on the tracks."

"But we can't!" Peg said. "A train might come. We could be killed!"

"Look back there," Bob told her. He pointed to the man who was still after them. "He has a knife."

Peg looked down at the tracks. "OK," she said. "Come on."

She climbed down the steps to the tracks. Bob climbed down after her.

He pointed to the third rail. "Don't touch that rail," he said. "If you do, you'll die. The third rail is full of electricity to run the trains. Stay close to the wall. Move fast."

Peg looked back as they went through the tunnel. "I don't see anyone after us," she said.

It was dark in the tunnel. But there were a few small lights. Some of the lights were red, some green. One or two were yellow.

"It's hard to see," Peg said. "How far do we have to go before—?"

The rest of her words couldn't be heard. The train made too much noise.

"Stop!" someone yelled.

Peg and Bob looked back. They saw that the man with the knife was still after them. He was on the tracks, too.

"Run!" Peg shouted to Bob at the top of her voice. "Run!"

They ran. The man ran after them. So did Baxter, who was also on the tracks.

Suddenly, a bright white light flashed in their eyes.

"It's another train!" Peg shouted. "It's coming this way!"

Bob grabbed her arm and pulled her back. "Get in here! Hurry, Peg!"

He pulled her close to him. Then he shoved her into a space in the wall. It was just big enough for both of them. They stood there as the train came down the track.

"Keep your back pressed up against the wall," Bob said. "Don't move an inch. Peg, can you hear me?"

"I hear you. I—"

The train came toward them. The noise it made was so loud that Peg couldn't even think. All she could do was press her back against the wall and hope. She could feel Bob's body next to her own.

It seemed to her that it took the train a year to pass.

When it was past them, she heard a man scream. "Bob!" she shouted.

"It wasn't me," he shouted back. "I'm OK. Come on! Let's get out of here."

Bob took her hand. Together, they ran down the track. Soon they came to another platform. It had bright lights on it. They climbed up the steps to the platform.

"Let's go over there," Peg said. "There are some chairs over there. I have to sit down. My legs feel weak."

They sat down on the chairs. They didn't say anything for several minutes.

Finally, Peg looked around her. She said, "Are we safe now?"

"To tell you the truth," Bob said, "I don't know. But I'll tell you what I think. I think we won't be safe as long as you have that statue."

"When we were in the subway tunnel—who screamed?"

"Maybe it was the man with the knife," Bob said.

"Or Mr. Baxter," Peg said.

"We had better get out of here now," Bob said. "Let's not wait for a train. Let's walk to the police station."

They got up. They climbed the subway steps up to the street.

"Which way do we go?" Peg asked.

Bob pointed down the street. They went that way, walking very fast.

Lights were coming on all over the city. It was almost dark. People were coming out of buildings. Some stores were already closed.

Peg looked up at the sky. There was so much light from the tall buildings that she couldn't see the stars.

She put her hands in her coat pockets.

And felt the statue.

Just then they went past a ten cent store. Peg suddenly had an idea.

"I'll be back in a minute," she said to Bob. She started into the store.

"Peg!" Bob yelled after her. "What are you doing? We haven't got time to shop for anything now. Later we can—"

But Peg was already inside the store. Bob stood outside. He looked through the window of the store. But he couldn't see Peg.

He was mad. Why did she have to shop now? he asked himself. Didn't she know that they might get hurt if—

Just then, Peg came out of the store. There was a big smile on her face.

"It's about time," Bob said. "Of all the silly things to do!"

"Please don't be mad at me," Peg said. "I didn't take long, did I?"

"No, but—"

"Let's go," she said. She looked behind her. "I think we got away from them," she told Bob.

But she was wrong.

As she and Bob stopped at a corner for a red light, she saw Baxter.

He was in a taxi that was coming down the street toward them.

The taxi stopped. Baxter jumped out of it.

CHAPTER **6**

A PLACE TO HIDE

"Bob!" Peg yelled. "It's Baxter!"

Bob and Peg began to run. Soon Peg was far ahead of Bob.

Suddenly, she stopped running. She went inside a big building. Bob came to the building and went inside, too.

"Come on," Peg said to him. "We have to find a place to hide."

"We should have gone to the police station," Bob said.

"I didn't think about that," Peg said. "When I saw Baxter—well, I was afraid. I just ran right in here."

"Don't worry about it now. Let's do as you said. Let's find some place to hide."

They looked around. They saw a sign that said: STAIRS.

They ran to the door under the sign. They went through the door and climbed the stairs. They climbed for a long time. At last, they went through another door. They came to a very large room.

There were desks in the room.

"This is some kind of an office building," Bob said. "It looks as if everyone has gone home for the day."

They saw a sign that said: STOREROOM.

"That's as good as any place to hide," Bob said. "Come on."

They went into the storeroom. It was full of boxes of all sizes.

"Let's hide behind that pile of boxes over there," Peg said.

They did. They sat down on the floor behind the boxes. They listened. They couldn't hear a sound.

"Do you think he saw us come into the building?" Peg asked.

"The candy man?"

"Yes, Baxter," Peg said. "Do you think—?"

"I don't know if he saw us or not. But we had better play it safe. Let's stay here for now."

"He won't find us here, will he?" Peg asked. "I mean if he is in the building, too?"

"I don't think he would have much of a chance," Bob said.

Peg wondered if Bob said that just so she wouldn't worry. She hoped not. She hoped she would never see Baxter again.

There was no noise in the building. Peg listened but she couldn't hear a thing. She looked at her watch. It was after six o'clock.

The next time she looked at her watch, it was almost seven o'clock.

"I think it would be safe to leave now," she said to Bob. "Don't you?"

"Let's give it a try."

Together they made their way to the door of the storeroom. They opened it.

They went to the stairs and then down them. It took them some time to get to the bottom of them.

As they came out on the first floor, Peg almost screamed.

"I've been waiting here for you," Baxter said. He was standing in the middle of the first floor. Behind him was the door to the street.

"I saw you come in here. So of course I came in, too. They have now closed the building for the night. I found a place to hide until everyone was gone. Now all the doors are locked."

"I don't believe you," Peg said.

"Try the front door for yourself," Baxter said. He stepped to one side.

Peg, watching him, went to the front door. She tried to open it. But she couldn't. It was locked. She went back to where Bob stood.

"We can't get out of here!" she whispered to him. "Baxter—for once he told the truth. The door really is locked. We are locked in here with him!"

"Do you still have the statue, my dear?" Baxter asked Peg.

Peg's hand slipped into her coat pocket.

"I see you do have it. How nice. How very nice. Felix would have been so pleased."

"Who is Felix?" Bob asked Baxter.

"He is—he *was*—a friend of mine," Baxter answered. "You two know him." To Peg, he said, "He was in your brother's apartment some hours ago."

"Where is he now?" Peg asked. She looked behind her.

"He isn't here now. I'm afraid Felix ran into a bit of trouble on the subway tracks. He didn't get out of the way of the train in time."

"Do you mean—?" Peg said.

"Felix is dead," Baxter said. "The train ran over him. But *I* am not dead. And I want that statue."

"Why do you want it?" Peg asked. "What good is it to you?"

Baxter laughed. "It's not really the statue itself that I want."

"Then what is it?" Peg asked.

"I want what is *inside* the statue."

"What *is* inside it?" Bob asked.

"Heroin," said Baxter. "Pure heroin. Heroin that I can sell on the street for more than a million dollars. Once it is cut, that is."

"Where did you get it?" Peg asked.

"I told you that I was a salesman," Baxter said. "My business happens to be selling heroin.

I knew that a man was going to bring some heroin from Chicago to New York. He had it inside a statue in his flight bag. So I bought a flight bag just like his. Then I switched the bags in the Chicago airport."

Peg's eyes opened wide in surprise. "That man who tried to take your flight bag in the Chicago airport—"

"He spoke the truth, my dear. It *was* his flight bag. And in it was the statue. I suppose he telephoned friends here in New York to watch out for me. When we got to New York, I saw a man—a man I knew. The man was a friend of the one in Chicago. He was waiting for me. All of us are in the same business. We pretty much know one another."

"That's when you asked me to get you a drink of water," Peg said. "But you didn't really want a drink of water. You wanted—"

"I wanted a chance, my dear," Baxter said. "A chance to slip the statue into your coat pocket. I made sure the man didn't see me do it. I knew the statue would be safe with you. I also knew I could follow you and get it back."

"You left your flight bag," Peg said. "The man took it from me. He thought the statue was still in the bag, didn't he?"

"I'm sure he did," Baxter said. "He was in for a surprise, wasn't he?"

Baxter began to laugh. Then he suddenly stopped laughing. "Now then," he said. He took a step toward Peg and Bob.

He said, "I've put all the elevators out of order. You can't get out of here. And you can't get away from me."

"How did you do that?" Bob asked him.

"I know how to do many interesting things," Baxter said. "I know how to put elevators out of order. I know how to get rich selling heroin. And I know how to kill people who make trouble for me. I may be fat but my fingers are strong."

He lifted his hands. He closed his fingers as if they were around someone's neck.

"Wait," Peg said. Her voice was so low that Bob could not hear her. "Don't do anything to us," she whispered. "I'll give you the statue if you'll just—"

Before she could say anything more, Bob yelled, "Come on, Peg!" He grabbed her hand and pulled her along with him.

They both ran toward the stairs.

CHAPTER **7**

FOOTSTEPS ON THE STAIRS

Through the door they ran and up the stairs.

They ran up ten flights of stairs. Then they stopped.

"Is he after us?" Peg asked. "Can you hear him down there?"

Bob listened for a minute. "I don't hear anything."

"I don't either," Peg said. "Maybe he won't follow us."

"Don't bet on it. He wants that statue. Maybe we should just give it to him."

"That's what I was going to do," Peg said. "But then you grabbed my hand and started to run. What was it?"

"I was afraid he would kill us anyway," Bob said. "But maybe it would be better to try it."

Peg closed her eyes. In her mind she could see Baxter's strong hands. They were coming toward her. They were on her neck. They were cutting off her air—her life.

She opened her eyes. "I know I could give him the statue," she said. "But I don't think I should. The more I think about it—no, I don't think I should."

"Why not?" Bob said.

"He would sell that heroin to a lot of people. Maybe even little kids. I have read about what heroin can do to people's lives. He would string out a lot of people. Change them so nothing in their lives matters but the next shot of heroin. Some of them might die. All of them would be turned into the living dead. No, I'm going to keep the statue. I'm going to give it to the police. Not to Baxter."

"Listen," Bob said. "Did you hear something?"

Peg listened. She heard what Bob had heard. Footsteps on the stairs.

"It's him," Bob said. "He is still after us."

"Let's climb the stairs," Peg said. "We can hide in one of the rooms of the building."

Bob tried the door beside him. "Locked," he said. "Let's try the next floor."

They ran up another flight of stairs. They tried the door there. It too was locked.

So was the door on the next floor.

"Let's go to the floor we were on before," Peg said. "That door is open."

They climbed more flights of stairs. Finally, they came to the door they had gone through before.

Bob opened it and they went into the room full of desks. "Let's hide in the storeroom again," he said.

Peg suddenly shook her head.

"No? Why not?"

"Probably all the doors below us are locked," Peg said. "So when Baxter gets to this floor, he will guess that we went inside this room. There is a good chance that he will find us if we hide here. He's pretty smart."

"Then what can we do?" Bob asked. "Do you have a better idea?"

"No, I don't," Peg said. "I just know that we should not hide in here. Let's keep going up. Let's see what happens."

"It's a big chance to take," Bob said.

"We have to take it. We have to hope it works out for us."

They left the room. They climbed the stairs. Below them, they could hear Baxter's footsteps on the stairs.

"He isn't coming after us very fast," Bob said.

"He doesn't have to. He knows we are trapped. There isn't any other way down."

As they reached each floor, they tried the doors on them. All the doors were locked.

Five minutes later, they reached the top of the stairs.

"Now what?" Bob said, looking all around. "Now where can we go?"

"Look," Peg said. "There is a door over there." She went over to it. "Bob, it's open!"

Peg opened the door. "That's the roof of the building out there."

They stepped out on the roof.

The building next door was just as tall as the one they were on.

"Shut that door," Peg told Bob.

He shut it. "If we could only lock it from this side," he said. He began to look around the roof. "I've found something," he yelled to Peg.

He brought back a big board. He put one end of the board against the door. The other one he put against the roof.

"Will that keep Baxter inside?" Peg asked her brother.

"I don't know. It might," Bob answered. "I sure do hope it does."

"So do I," Peg said. She walked to the edge of the roof. She looked down at the street far below.

The people on the street looked tiny.

She looked up at the sky. Now she could see the stars because it was dark on top of the building. The stars seemed close enough to touch.

She looked at the building next door. Between the two buildings was a space of almost six feet.

She looked down between the two buildings. If I fell down there, she thought, I would die for sure. I wouldn't have a chance.

She looked back at the door. The board was still against it.

Bob said, "Did that board move? I thought it did. But I'm not sure if it did or not."

Peg looked at the board. She saw it move.

Bob ran over to it. He put his foot on it. But the board moved again. The handle of the door turned.

Bob put all of his weight against the door. For several seconds, nothing happened.

But suddenly someone bumped against the door from inside the building.

Bob tried to hold the door shut. But he couldn't. It flew open. The board fell to the roof with a bang.

Through the door came Baxter.

"So we meet again," he said. "But I must say that I don't like this game of ours. Even as a child, I didn't like to play games."

Bob backed away from him. And then, suddenly, he grabbed the board that was on the roof. He tried to hit Baxter with it.

But Baxter saw what he was going to do. He moved fast for a fat man. He moved as fast as a cat after a bird.

The board in Bob's hands came down. But it only hit the roof.

Baxter kicked the board out of Bob's hands. He grabbed Bob by the neck.

He didn't say anything at all. He just held on to Bob's neck.

Bob tried hard to fight. But Baxter's hands didn't let go.

"Stop it!" Peg yelled. "Please stop it!"

But Baxter didn't stop it. He held on to Bob's neck. Bob's face turned red, then blue.

And then, at last, he let go.

Bob fell to the roof. He didn't move at all.

Baxter looked down at him. And then he looked over at Peg. "Now then, my dear," he said. "I think it is time for the two of us to do business. Don't you?"

Peg didn't say anything at first. But then she said, "You win."

She put her hand in her coat pocket. "If I give you the statue, will you let us go?"

"Of course," said Baxter. "I don't want you. Or your brother who tried to kill me. Just the heroin. Did I tell you that many people like heroin even better than I like candy? Don't ask me why. But they do."

He held out his hand.

Peg took the statue out of her pocket. Very slowly she walked over to Baxter. Very slowly she gave the statue to him.

CHAPTER **8**

OUR ONLY CHANCE

"Thank you, my dear," Baxter said.

He put the statue in his pocket. From his other pocket he took a piece of candy. He ate it.

Peg got down on the roof. She touched Bob's face. It felt cold. "You killed him," she said.

"No, he is not dead," Baxter said. "He will soon be fine. I didn't kill him. But I could have. So you have something to thank me for, don't you?" He ate another piece of candy.

"Go away," Peg said. "You have the statue. Please just go away now."

"I shall do just that," Baxter said. "Take good care of your brother. Good-bye."

He turned and went through the door and down the steps.

"Bob," Peg said. "Bob, can you hear me?"

Bob said nothing. He didn't move.

Peg spoke his name a second time.

Some minutes later, he opened his eyes. He gave Peg a weak smile. Then he looked all around him.

"Baxter is gone," Peg said to him. "I gave him the statue and he left."

"But you said you wouldn't give it to him," Bob said.

"I know I said that. But I had to give it to him. I really did. Now we can leave."

Bob stood up. He went to the door and listened. "I can't hear anything. I guess he really is gone."

"Bob!" Peg said. "I just thought of something—something bad."

"What?"

"Baxter can't get out of the building. The front door is locked."

"I know. But that's not a problem, is it? We can stay up here. And he can stay down there. I mean until morning comes and they open the building."

"Yes, it is a problem," Peg said. "It's a big problem for us."

"I don't understand you, Peg."

"Let me explain. I told you that I gave the statue to Baxter."

"So? Get to the point."

"I will. The statue I gave him—well, it was—it wasn't—"

Bob put up a hand. Peg stopped speaking.

"I hear footsteps on the stairs," he said. "They aren't going down. They are coming *up!*"

"I knew it!" Peg whispered. "It's Baxter!"

"What do you mean?"

"Never mind now. I'll tell you later. Right now we have to get off this roof."

"But you know we can't," Bob said. "Not unless we can get past Baxter. We can't—"

"We *can!*" Peg said.

"How? I don't see how. There is no *way* we can get off this roof."

"Come with me," Peg said. She took Bob's hand. They went to the edge of the roof.

"We can jump," she said.

Bob looked at her in complete surprise. "You mean jump from this roof to that one over there?"

"We have to try it," Peg said. "It's our only chance."

"But that other building is almost six feet away. We could fall. If we fell, we would be killed."

Bob stepped back from the edge of the roof. "You gave Baxter the statue. That's all he wants. He won't hurt us now."

"Yes, I have the statue," Baxter said as he came through the door. "But it is not the statue I want."

"I really don't know what this is all about," Bob said.

"I'm not sure I do either," Baxter said. "But I just checked the statue your sister gave me. It isn't *my* statue. Mine was full of heroin. This one is empty inside."

He held up the statue Peg had given him. He threw it down on the roof. It broke.

"Now I want *my* statue," he said. He began to move toward them. "And I want it now. Where is it? Did you hide it?"

"Bob," Peg whispered, "we have to do it."

She walked toward Baxter. Then she suddenly turned around. She began to run. She jumped from the roof. She landed on the roof of the building next door.

"Bob," she yelled. "Come on. Jump!"

Bob looked down at the ground far below.

"Don't do that!" Peg shouted at him. "Don't look down. *Jump!*"

Bob backed away from the edge of the roof.
Baxter ran toward him.

Bob jumped.

He landed on the roof next door beside Peg.
He just made it by inches.

Baxter let out an angry yell. He was coming
after them.

Peg ran to the door on the roof. "It's open, Bob. Come on."

She looked back. She saw Baxter jump from the roof she had been on. But he was too fat to make it. She heard him scream as he fell down between the two buildings.

She covered her face with her hands.

Bob put his arms around her. "It's all over," he said. "Take it easy, OK?"

Peg didn't say anything. She couldn't speak.

"Where did that statue that you gave Baxter come from?" he asked Peg.

At last, she looked up at him. She almost smiled. "Do you remember when I went into that ten cent store before?"

"Yes, I do."

"I went in to see if they had any statues like Baxter's for sale. They did. I bought one. That was the one I gave to him."

Surprise showed on Bob's face. Then he began to smile. "You are some smart sister!" he said.

Peg put her hand in her coat pocket. She took out Baxter's statue. "Now we can take this one to the police."

Bob looked at his watch. "In a few more hours, I can wish you a happy birthday."

"Do it now," Peg said.

"Happy birthday, beautiful," Bob said.

"Thank you," Peg said. "Thank you very much, big brother."

"And welcome to New York City," Bob said.

"Mr. Baxter didn't make me feel very welcome," Peg said.

"But I did," Bob said. "Isn't that enough?"

"That's more than enough," Peg said.